Toby

Safely Home

BY JOY ROBERTS

Illustrated by
JOY ROBERTS and ERIN LEUCI

XULON PRESS

Xulon Press
2301 Lucien Way #415
Maitland, FL 32751
407.339.4217
www.xulonpress.com

Printed in the United States of America.

Paperback ISBN-13: 978-1-6628-0364-2
Hard Cover ISBN-13: 978-1-6628-0365-9
Ebook ISBN-13: 978-1-6628-0366-6

This book is dedicated to Jesus Christ,
for giving me the gift of *Toby*
to help my children and
so many others have peace in times of loss.

CONTENTS

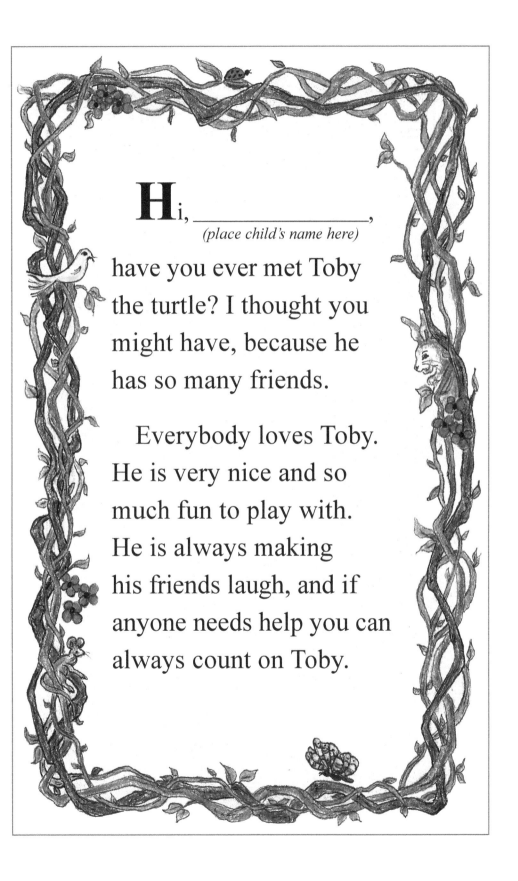

Hi, _____,
have you ever met Toby
the turtle? I thought you
might have, because he
has so many friends.

Everybody loves Toby.
He is very nice and so
much fun to play with.
He is always making
his friends laugh, and if
anyone needs help you can
always count on Toby.

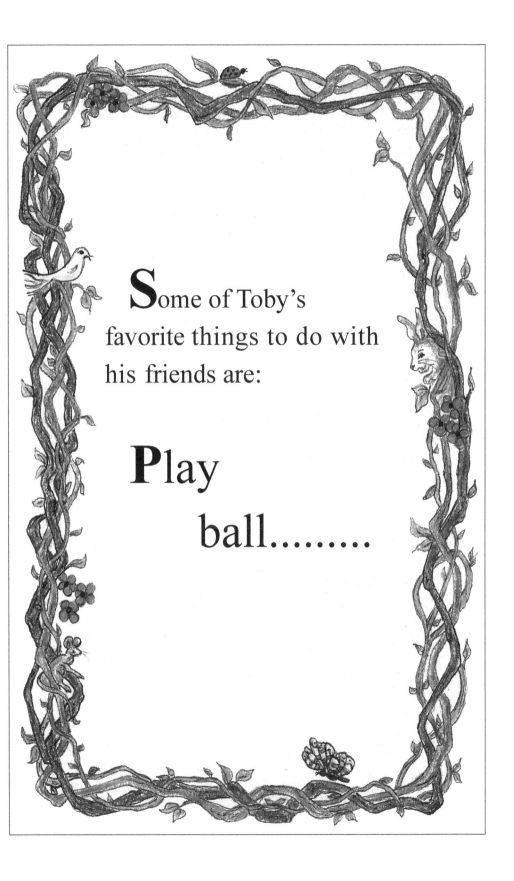

Some of Toby's favorite things to do with his friends are:

Play

ball.........

Swim in the
pond.........

Ride

bikes..........

Eat Farmer Bernard's dark green grassy grass in the meadow, or just lay in the summer noon day sun.

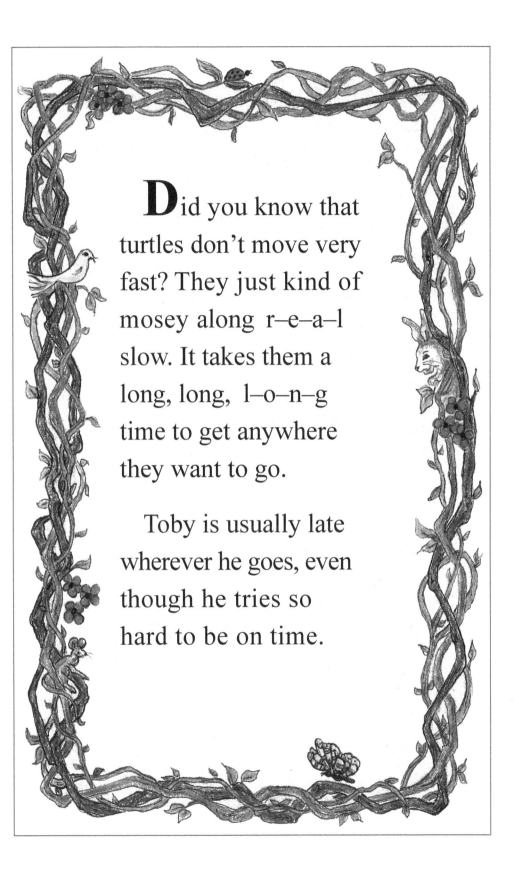

Did you know that turtles don't move very fast? They just kind of mosey along r–e–a–l slow. It takes them a long, long, l–o–n–g time to get anywhere they want to go.

Toby is usually late wherever he goes, even though he tries so hard to be on time.

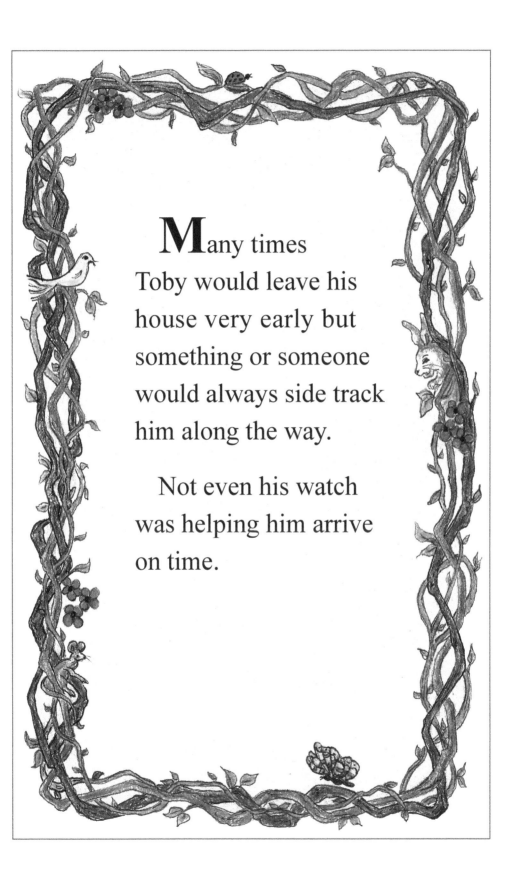

Many times Toby would leave his house very early but something or someone would always side track him along the way.

Not even his watch was helping him arrive on time.

Often someone would stop Toby to talk, and he couldn't hurt their feelings by not stopping to talk to them.

And, if someone needed Toby's help he would always take time to give them a helping hand.

One hot summer day as Toby was crossing the field to get to his favorite place in Farmer Bernard's dark green grassy meadow, the tractor came around the bend very fast!

Too fast for Toby to get out of the way!

The tractor STRUCK Toby HARD... and he died!

When Toby's friends heard that he was gone, they all cried because they were so sad.

They knew they would never see him here on earth again, and they were going to miss Toby so much.

If only Toby's friends could have seen the beautiful angels come and take his soul up to heaven. They would have seen how much fun he was having, and how happy he was flying up through the clouds.

Then they would have been so happy for him! It would have made them feel so much better and made it much easier for them to let him go.

As Toby floated up to the sky he thought, "Hey, this is fun!"

He felt so different, so light... like he was flying. Oh, but he was flying!

Up, up, and away, higher and higher up into the sky, as the angels led him up to his heavenly home.

All of Toby's family and friends who had died before him were waiting there, along with God's son Jesus and the angels.

They had a great big party to welcome Toby to heaven because everyone was so excited to have him with them

Safely Home.

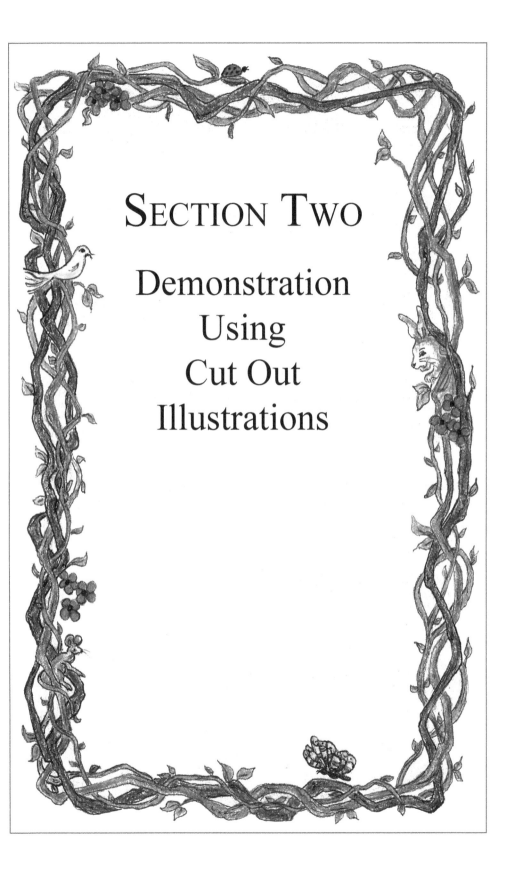

SECTION TWO

Demonstration
Using
Cut Out
Illustrations

Section Two

Demonstration Using Illustrations

Cut out Characters before reading

Everyone's body has a soul. Your soul lives inside your body, it's like a house for your soul.

Step 1: Place the turtle's body on top of the turtle's soul.

The turtle's shell is the house that his soul lives in. When the turtle dies his house stays here but his soul leaves his house and goes up to live in heaven.

Step 2: Take the shell off of the soul and set it aside. Make the soul go upward towards heaven.

The turtle is still alive, but now he is living in heaven. No one's soul ever dies, you just don't get to see them here on earth anymore where we live.

Step 3: Place the man's body on top of his soul. Demonstrate with the body just as you did with the turtle's shell. Show the body staying here dead, and raise the soul up alive towards heaven.

It's the same way with people. Our body is the house that our soul lives in. You can't see our soul but it is living inside of us. When a person dies their body stays here and their soul goes on to live in heaven with Jesus and it will never die.

Cut Out

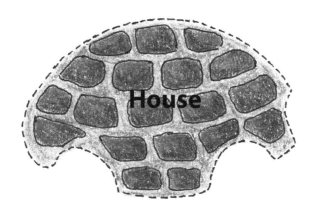

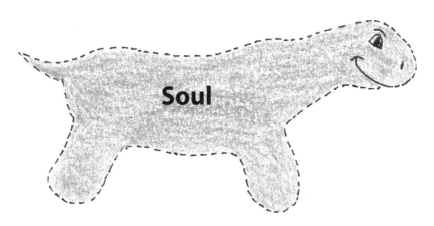

Cut Out

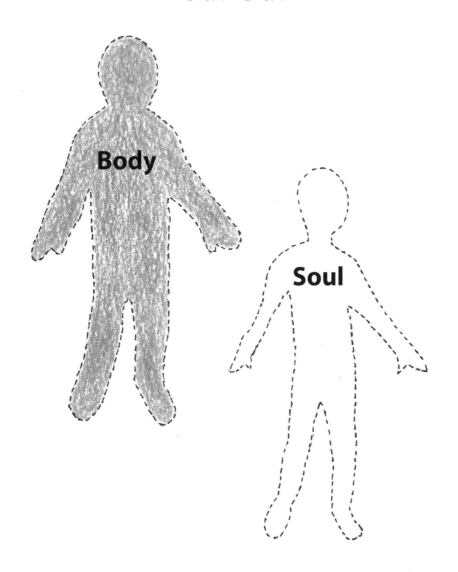

SECTION THREE

Explanation
of Heaven

SECTION THREE

Explanation of Heaven

Heaven is a wonderful place full of love, peace, and joy. There is no pain, sorrow, or sickness, not even one tear. Everyone is happy every single day. If your loved one was sick when they died, they are completely without any kind of sickness or pain now that they are in heaven. But the best part of heaven is, that God and Jesus are there and they will be with your loved one forever. God and Jesus will always be there to take care of them.

Your loved ones in heaven are happy. They are looking forward to the day when your journey here on earth is done, so you can all be together again.

It's okay to cry because you've lost someone or something that you love very much. Maybe someone close to you like a friend, family member, or even a pet that you loved has died. It's good to talk to someone about how you're feeling and how much you miss the person or pet. It's important to talk to Jesus too, because he really cares that you are sad and hurting. He wants to help you through this time of sadness.

It will take time, but some day you will feel better and eventually the hurt will go away. You will always have the memory of them and they will always be in your heart.

CPSIA information can be obtained
at www.ICGtesting.com
Printed in the USA
BVHW091543140121
597833BV00002B/2